The
Speedy Tortoise

First published in 2010
by Wayland

This paperback edition published in 2011 by Wayland
Published under a different series title in hardback

Wayland
338 Euston Road
London NW1 3BH

Wayland Australia
Level 17/207 Kent Street
Sydney, NSW 2000

Series Editor: Louise John
Editor: Katie Powell
Cover design: Paul Cherrill
Design: D.R.ink
Consultant: Shirley Bickler

A CIP catalogue record for this book is available from the British Library.

ISBN 9780750266062

Printed in China

Wayland is a division of Hachette Children's Books,
an Hachette UK Company

www.hachette.co.uk

The Speedy Tortoise

Written by Joe Hackett
Illustrated by Mike Spoor

WAYLAND

Tessie the tortoise was in a spot of bother at Animal School.

She was lying helplessly on her back in the middle of the playground, with her legs waving in the air.

"Help!" Tessie shouted. "I've had an accident."

Tessie's friends rushed to her side.

"Not again," said Robert the rhino.
"What on earth happened?"

"I was racing to the classroom and
I tripped over a rock on the ground,"
said Tessie. "I can't get up."

Tessie was a very ordinary sort of tortoise, except for one thing. Tessie didn't plod along slowly, as tortoises usually do. She raced everywhere as fast as she could. It got her into all sorts of scrapes.

Everyone pushed and pulled. At last,
with a big heave-ho, Tessie rolled onto
her front again, but there was a nasty
scratch on her shell.

"Oh, no, I've scratched my shell!"
Tessie moaned.

Just then, the bell rang for class to begin and everyone went inside.

Tessie forgot all about her scratched shell and whizzed straight into the classroom at top speed, almost knocking her friends over.

"Watch out!" croaked Finlay the frog, as Tessie charged past him to get to her desk. "I thought tortoises were supposed to be slow."

"Oh, I'm sorry, Finlay. I wish I could slow down sometimes," Tessie said. "But I just get too impatient!"

"The trouble is, Tessie, you race so fast that you hurt yourself," said Latif the lion, looking at Tessie's scratched shell. "One day you might really do some damage."

"I know," said Tessie, miserably.
"But I just can't seem to remember
to slow down!"

At that moment, Mrs Hooper, the teacher, came in and saw Tessie's shell.

"Goodness me! Look at that big scratch. You've been dashing about again, Tessie," she said. "You speed around here like a racing car!"

And that was what gave Oliver the owl an idea.

"Yes, Tessie! You're exactly like a car!" he hooted. "And do you know what signal makes a car stop?"

"Of course, I do," mumbled Tessie.
"Cars stop when traffic lights are
on red."

"Yes! So, if we put up red signs at places where there's danger, you'll remember to slow down and stop. Just like a car does," said Oliver.

"That's a great idea!" said Latif the lion.

"Brilliant!" croaked Finlay.

"OK, everyone, let's make some red traffic lights," said Mrs Hooper.

The class got some paper and
painted bright red circles on it.
Then they began looking around
the school for dangerous places.

"Here's a dangerous place," said Patty the pig. "You might fall down these stairs if you run too fast."

Patty taped a red circle at the top of the staircase.

"And here's another tricky spot," said Latif, looking at the rock in the playground that Tessie had tripped over that same morning.

Soon, there were red circles all over the school.

"All you need to do, Tessie, is remember to stop when you see a red circle," said Mrs Hooper.

Tessie nodded. "OK, I'll try."

Tessie set off. First she came to the stairs. She saw the red sign and stopped. Tessie even remembered to look left and right before she raced off again.

Then, Tessie raced towards a sharp corner of the school building. She saw the red sign and stopped.

And everyone clapped and cheered
when Tessie remembered to stop at
the rock in the playground, too!

"Thank you, everyone!" she cried.
"It's much easier to remember to
stop when I see a red circle."

At that moment the bell rang
for the end of the school day.

Tessie looked up and began to
laugh. There, on the stretch of grass
leading to the school gates, Mrs
Hooper had put up a green circle!

As quick as a flash, Tessie raced towards the gates without even waving goodbye to her friends.

"Green for 'GO'!" shouted Tessie.
"Now I can run."

"Here comes my girl. The fastest
tortoise in town!" Tessie's dad called
out, laughing. "Watch out, everyone!"

START READING is a series of highly enjoyable books for beginner readers. **The books have been carefully graded to match the Book Bands widely used in schools.** This enables readers to be sure they choose books that match their own reading ability.

Look out for the Band colour on the book in our Start Reading logo.

The Bands are:

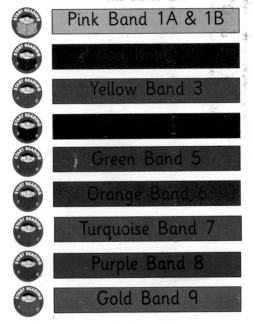

Pink Band 1A & 1B

Red Band 2

Yellow Band 3

Green Band 5

Orange Band 6

Turquoise Band 7

Purple Band 8

Gold Band 9

START READING books can be read independently or shared with an adult. They promote the enjoyment of reading through satisfying stories supported by fun illustrations.

Joe Hackett was born on a farm. He remembers riding on a horse so big that he couldn't get his legs across its back. Now he lives on a little farm again, with his wife and dog Ozzie, who is small, black and brown, and loves best of all to go down badger and rabbit holes.

Mike Spoor loves being able to spend his days drawing the animals and pets of his childhood. He especially likes drawing animals with personalities that can be captured in his drawings, such as Latif the lion, Patty the pig, Finlay the frog and Tessie the tortoise.